las diez campanas

la vaca

la bota

el pie

las cinco niñas

una niña

el dedo
↓
la mano

un niño

la silla

los cuatro niños

los tres caracoles

las nueve flores

el cerdo

La Madre Goose

NURSERY RHYMES
for LOS NIÑOS

Susan Middleton Elya

illustrated by **Juana Martinez-Neal**

G. P. PUTNAM'S SONS

To my mom, Joanne
—S.M.E.

For my three:
Ethan, Aidan and Eva
—J.M–N.

G. P. PUTNAM'S SONS
an imprint of Penguin Random House LLC
375 Hudson Street
New York, NY 10014

Library of Congress Cataloging-in-Publication Data
Elya, Susan Middleton, 1955– author.
La Madre Goose : nursery rhymes for los niños / Susan
Middleton Elya ; illustrated by Juana Martinez-Neal.
pages cm   In English with some Spanish words.
Summary: A collection of classic nursery rhymes presented
with a bilingual twist. 1. Nursery rhymes. 2. Children's
poetry. 3. Stories in rhyme. [1. Nursery rhymes. 2. Spanish
language—Vocabulary—Fiction.] I. Martinez-Neal, Juana,
illustrator. II. Mother Goose. III. Title.
PZ8.3.E514Mad 2016   398.8—dc23   2014040375
Manufactured in China by
RR Donnelley Asia Printing Solutions Ltd.
ISBN 978-0-399-25157-3
10 9 8 7 6 5 4 3

Design by Annie Ericsson. Text set in Maiandra.
The art was created with acrylics, colored pencils
and graphite on handmade textured paper.

Glossary

(la)	**alegría** (ah leh GREE ah) joy	
	amarilla (ah mah REE yah) yellow	
(la)	**araña** (ah RAH nyah) spider	
(la)	**arañita** (ah rah NYEE tah) small spider	
(el)	**armario** (ahr MAH ryoe) cupboard	
(el)	**arroz** (ah RROCE) rice	
(el)	**azúcar** (ah SOO kahr) sugar	
	azul (ah SOOL) blue	
	bella (BEH yah) beautiful	
(el)	**beso** (BEH soe) kiss	
	bonita (boe NEE tah) pretty	
	buenos (BWEH noce) good	
(la)	**calabaza** (kah lah BAH sah) pumpkin	
(las)	**campanas** (kahm PAH nahs) bells	
(los)	**caracoles** (kah rah KOE lehs) snails	
(la)	**carne** (KAHR neh) meat	
(la)	**casa** (KAH sah) house	
(la)	**casita** (kah SEE tah) little house	
(el)	**cerdo** (SEHR doe) pig	
	cinco (SEEN koe) five	
(los)	**colores** (koe LOE rehs) colors	
(las)	**conchas blancas** (KONE chahs BLAHN kahs) white shells	
(las)	**culebras** (koo LEH brahs) snakes	
	de (DEH) of	
(el)	**dedo** (DEH doe) finger	
(el)	**diamante** (dyah MAHN teh) diamond	

domingo (doe MEEN goe) Sunday

dos (DOSE) two

el (EHL) the (masculine singular)

en el rincón (EHN EHL rreen KONE)
  in the corner

(la) **estrella** (ehs TREH yah) star

extraña (ehks TRAH nyah) strange

(las) **flores** (FLOE rehs) flowers

(la) **fortuna** (fohr TOO nah) fortune

(los) **frijoles** (free HOE lehs) beans

(los) **gatitos** (gah TEE toce) kittens

(el, los) **gato, gatos** (GAH toe, GAH toce)
  cat, cats

(el) **hueso** (WEH soe) bone

(el) **jardín** (hahr DEEN) garden

jueves (HWEH vehs) Thursday

la (LAH) the (feminine singular)

las (LAHS) the (feminine plural)

(la) **lana** (LAH nah) wool

llenas (YEH nahs) full

(la) **lluvia** (YOO vyah) rain

los (LOS) the (masculine plural)

(la) **luna** (LOO nah) moon

lunes (LOO nehs) Monday

(la) **madre** (MAH dreh) mother

malos (MAH loce) bad

Mami (MAH mee) Mommy

martes (MAHR tehs) Tuesday

mi (MEE) my

miao (MYOW) meow

miércoles (MYEHR koe lehs) Wednesday

(los) **mitoncitos** (mee tone SEE toce) mittens

(la, las) **niña, niñas** (NEE nyah, NEE nyahs)
  girl, girls

(el) **niño** (NEE nyoe) boy

(los) **niños** (NEE nyoce) boys, children

olé (oe LEH) bravo! good!

(la) **oveja** (oe VEH hah) sheep

(el) **padre** (PAH dreh) father

(las) **papas** (PAH pahs) potatoes

(el) **perro** (PEH rroe) dog

(el) **plato** (PLAH toe) plate

sábado (SAH bah doe) Saturday

seis (SAYCE) six

(las) **señoritas** (seh nyoe REE tahs) maidens,
  girls

sí (SEE) yes

siete (SYEH teh) seven

(la) **silla** (SEE yah) chair

(el) **sol** (SOLE) sun

(el) **toreador** (toe reh ah DOHR) bullfighter

(la) **torta** (TOHR tah) pie

tres (TREHS) three

un, una (OON, OO nah) a, an, one

(la) **vaca** (VAH kah) cow

vibrante (vee BRAHN teh) vibrant

viernes (VYEHR nehs) Friday

(la) **voz** (VOCE) voice

María Had a Little Oveja

María had a little **oveja**.
Its **lana** was white as snow.
And everywhere that María went,
  la oveja was sure to go.
It followed her to school one day,
  which was against the rule.
It made **los niños** laugh and play
  to see **una oveja** at school.

Baa, Baa, Black Oveja

Baa, baa, black **oveja**, have you any **lana**?
Sí, sir, **sí**, sir, three bags **llenas**.
One for my sister, **una** for **mi madre**,
and one to be shared by my brother and **mi padre**!

This Little *Cerdo* Went to Market

This little **cerdo** went to market,
　this little **cerdo** stayed home.
This little **cerdo** had roasted **carne**,
　this little **cerdo** had none.
This little **cerdo** cried oink, oink, oink,
　all the way home.

Three Little *Gatitos*

Three little **gatitos**
lost their **mitoncitos**
and they began to cry.
"Oh, **Mami** dear, we sadly fear
   our mittens have been lost."
"Lost your mittens, you **gatos malos**,
   then you shall have no **torta**."
"*Miao, miao, miao!*"

The little **gatitos**
found their **mitoncitos**
and they began to cry,
"Oh, **Mami** dear, see here, see here,
    our mittens have been found."
"What? Found your mittens,
    you **gatos buenos**,
    then you shall have some **torta**."
"Purr, purr, purr."

Peter, Peter Calabaza

Peter, Peter **Calabaza**,
got a wife for his new **casa**.
When she saw the round **casita**,
she repainted it—**bonita**!

María, María, Without Alegría

María, María, without *alegría*,
how does your *jardín* grow?
With silver *campanas*, and *conchas blancas*,
and *señoritas* all in a row.

Little Miss Amarilla

Miss **Amarilla** sat in her **silla**,
eating her beans and **arroz**.
There came a big **araña**
that was very **extraña**.
She screamed in a very loud **voz**!

Young Juan Ramón

Young Juan Ramón
sat **en el rincón**,
eating his green guacamole.
He put in his **dedo**,
pulled out a tomato,
and said, "Bring me rice and **frijoles**!"

Monday's Niño

El niño de lunes is fair of face.
El niño de martes is full of grace.
El niño de miércoles, full of woe.
El niño de jueves has far to go.
El niño de viernes is loving and giving.
El niño de sábado works for a living.
But the child that is born on **domingo** day
will be **un toreador**. *¡Olé!*

One Potato, Dos Potatoes

One potato, *dos* potatoes,
   tres potatoes, four.
Cinco papas, *seis papas*,
   siete papas, more!

Little Boy *Azul*

Little Boy **Azul**, come blow your horn.
La oveja's in the meadow, **la vaca**'s in the corn.
Where is **el niño** who looks after the sheep?
He is in the haystack, fast asleep.

Old Madre Rosario

Old **Madre** Rosario went to **el armario**
to get her poor dog **un hueso**.
But when she got there, **el armario** was bare,
so she gave her poor dog **un beso**.

The Itsy Arañita

The itsy *arañita*
    climbed up the water spout.
Down came *la lluvia* and
    washed *la araña* out.
Out came *el sol* and
    dried up all the rain,
and the itsy *arañita*
    went up the spout again.

What Are *las Niñas* Made Of?

What are **las niñas** made of?
What are **las niñas** made of?
Azúcar and **flores**
and all **los colores**.
That's what **las niñas** are made of!

What Are *los Niños* Made Of?

What are *los niños* made of?
What are *los niños* made of?
Culebras, *caracoles*
and jumping *frijoles*.
That's what *los niños* are made of!

Hey, Diddle, Diddle

Hey, diddle, diddle,
el gato and the fiddle,
la vaca jumped over *la luna*.
El perro laughed
to see such sport,
and *el plato* stole *una fortuna*.

Twinkle, Twinkle, Small *Estrella*

Twinkle, twinkle, small *estrella*,
how I wonder why you're **bella**.
Shining high, you're so **vibrante**,
in the sky *un diamante*.
Twinkle, twinkle, small *estrella*,
how I wonder why you're **bella**.

I See *la Luna*

I see *la luna*,
la luna sees me.
God bless *la luna*,
and God bless me.

las dos ovejas

la oveja   la ovejita

la luna

el pajarito

la casita

la arañita

la manzana

el gato

los siete cubos

la calabaza

el hueso

el perro   el plato

la estrellita

la estrella

el diamante

las ocho estrellas

los seis pollitos   el pollito